The Storytelling Princess

Rafe Martin

illustrated by

Kimberly Bulcken Root

G. P. Putnam's Sons • New York

Library of Congress Cataloging-in-Publication Data
Martin, Rafe, 1946–   The storytelling princess / by Rafe Martin ; illustrated by Kimberly Bulcken Root.
p. cm.   Summary: Having survived a shipwreck, a princess tries to tell a prince a story whose
ending he does not know and thus qualify for his hand in marriage. [1. Princes—Fiction.
2. Princesses—Fiction. 3. Storytelling—Fiction.] I. Root, Kimberly Bulcken, ill. II. Title.
PZ7.M3641835 Lo 2001   [E]—dc21   98-4335
ISBN 0-399-22924-8   10 9 8 7 6 5 4 3 2

For Mrs. Goldschlager, my first-grade teacher,
who told me I read aloud with expression —R. M.

For Barry —K. B. R.

ONCE there was a prince whose father, the king, one day said to him, "My boy, the time has come for you to marry. I've chosen the perfect princess for you. She lives far away, across the ocean, in a distant kingdom."

"No, Father," answered the prince. "I will only marry the princess I pick for myself."

And they had quite a discussion about it.

"All right," said the prince at last, "I'll marry her—on one condition. You must find someone who can tell me a story whose ending I don't know."

The king thought, "This will be hard. He knows so many stories. But I'll offer a big reward. Surely someone will come along who will be able to do it."

And so it was agreed.

FAR away, across the ocean, in a distant kingdom, there lived a princess. One day her father, the king, said to her, "My girl, you're grown. It's time you were married. And I've picked the perfect prince for you. His father and I have arranged it all."

But the princess said: "Absolutely not. I will never, never, *never* marry any prince but the prince I choose for myself. I'd rather be washed overboard in a storm at sea."

WE'LL see about that," stormed her father. And that very night the princess and her mother and father boarded their royal ship and set sail across the ocean.

ALL went smoothly, until one day there was a terrible storm.
A huge wave burst open the windows of the princess's room and
washed her out into the foaming sea!

SHE called for help.

But who could hear her in a storm like that?

The princess swam and swam. Just as her strength
seemed gone, her hand hit something hard. It was a trunk, washed
from the deck of the royal ship. The princess climbed on, held
tight, and fell fast asleep.

WHEN the princess awoke, the sun was shining. The trunk had come to rest on a beach. She was lost, hungry, alone. And curious. What was inside the trunk?

TAKING up a rock, she hammered open the lid. Inside, dry and clean, was a suit of sailor's clothes. Her dress was soaking wet, so she changed into the sailor's clothes. A pouch of silver coins lay in the chest, too, and she stuck that in her pocket. She put her hair up, put the sailor's hat on her head, and set off.

IN time she came to a big city.

She found an inn, where she ordered a hearty meal. When she finished she looked up, and there, nailed to a wall, was this proclamation:

Anyone who can tell my son, the prince,
a story whose ending he does not know
will receive a great, big reward!
—THE KING

"Aha," thought the princess. "I know lots of stories. I'll go to the palace and tell the cute little prince a story whose ending he doesn't know. I'll win the prize, buy a ship, and hire a crew. I'll sail home victoriously, and show my father that I know a thing or two!" So off she went.

SHE was ushered into the prince's throne room. But no cute
little prince sat there. It was a prince just about her own age.

The prince, seeing only a young sailor, looked up from his
book and said, "You think you can tell me a story whose
ending I don't know? Well, you can't. I've read so many
stories. No one can tell me anything surprising anymore.
You might as well weigh anchor right now, mate, and sail away."

"Shiver me timbers," answered the princess, "I'm a sailor, I've been before the mast, across the Line, and around the Horn. I've sailed the Seven Seas while you've just sat here on your throne. You'll never guess the ending of my tale."

"Really," said the prince. "Just listen to this." And bing, bang, bam, he began to reel off the names of story after story after story.

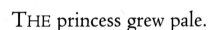

THE princess grew pale.

He had named all the stories she had ever read, ever heard, or ever dreamed of! What could she tell him? After a moment she had it. She told him this:

"Once there was a princess who sailed across the ocean. During the voyage there was a terrible storm. Lightning flashed. Thunder crashed. A huge wave broke against the ship, burst open the windows, and washed the princess out into the sea! She screamed and cried for help. But no one heard her and the ship sailed on.

"The storm was terrible," continued the princess. "Whales were tossed about like goldfish. Boats were spun around like chips of bark. The sea seethed and boiled! But even the worst storm must pass. In time this storm, too, drifted away. There she was, alone in the middle of the cold, green, vast, empty sea. Then what do you think she did?"

"Perhaps she swam?" offered the prince.

"YOU'RE right," agreed the princess. "She swam and swam and swam and swam. She was so tired she thought she would sink like a stone in the sea, when her hand hit something hard. What do you think it was?"

"Why, a rock, of course," said the prince.

"No."

"Why, then, a boat."

"No."

"A whale?"

"Nice try. But it wasn't a rock or a boat or a whale, or even a turtle."

"What, then?" asked the prince, sitting up on his throne.

"It was a trunk," she said, "a sailor's trunk, which had washed off the deck of the very ship she had been on. The princess climbed on the trunk and . . ."

"Wait a minute!" exclaimed the prince. "You really expect me—a grown-up, intelligent, well-educated human being—to believe that? It's preposterous! How could a trunk from her own ship just drift to where she was, when she had to swim and swim and swim to get there? Things like that don't happen in real life! You should do more research! But," he added, calming down a bit, "I . . . I like it. So go on with the story."

"I WILL," said the princess. "As I was saying, the princess climbed up on the trunk and fell asleep. When she awoke, the trunk was resting on a beach and the sun was shining. She didn't know where she was, what kingdom she was in. She was lost, hungry, alone. And curious. What was in the trunk? She hammered the trunk open with a rock, lifted the lid, and there, inside, and clean and dry, was a suit of sailor's clothes. And . . . and that's where we'll end our story for today."

"IT'S unusual," said the prince. "But there's something familiar about it, too. And you tell it well, with real expression, almost as if you had been there yourself. I like that. I'm not yet sure of the ending. But I'll get it. Come back tomorrow and tell me more."

"Don't worry," said the princess. "I'll be back."

And when she left the palace she knew what the ending of her tale was going to be. It was simple. The ending of her tale was that *this* was the prince she was going to marry. "I like him," she thought. "He's a great listener, and he appreciates a good story. I'll never marry that royal fool my father's picked."

FOR six days the princess returned to the palace and told the prince more of her own adventures as she wandered through the city in her disguise of sailor's clothes.

By the seventh day she knew the time had come to end her tale. Her money was gone, and she wanted to get safely to the ending now, where the prince and princess finally marry. Once, when the prince had exclaimed, "Oh, but I should like to meet such an adventurous princess as this!" she had almost stopped and told him the truth. But as she was determined to win the prize as well as the prince, and because she was enjoying herself so much, on she had gone with her story.

AT this very time a ship sailed into the harbor. After days of fruitless tacking and yawing over the blue ocean in search of their daughter, the lost princess, the king and queen had finally arrived to tell their sad tale.

THEY went to the palace and tearfully told the prince's mother and father the terrible news: their dear daughter, the royal princess, had been washed overboard and lost at sea.

"How horrible," sobbed the prince's father and mother, blowing their royal noses in their royal handkerchiefs.

AND down the hall they all went,
to tell the prince that his bride-to-be
had been lost at sea.

NOW, at that very moment, inside the prince's throne room, the princess was telling the prince this: "And then the princess, in her suit of sailor's clothes, went to the palace and told the prince a story whose ending he didn't know."

THE prince's eyes opened wide. "Wait a minute!" he exclaimed as he leapt from his throne. "I've got it! I've got the ending of the story! *You* are the princess!"

"Yes," cried the princess. "But that's still not the *end* of the story." And as she said this she took off the sailor's clothes. "The ending of this story is that the prince and the princess get mar—"

JUST then the door swung open and in stepped her mother and father. When her mother saw her daughter she cried, "My dear g—!" and fainted to the ground. Her father ran forward, crying, "My dear girl, *alive*!"

WELL, the princess and the prince did get married. But neither had gotten the ending of the story quite right. They were each marrying the person they had chosen to marry, but neither had guessed they were also marrying the very one they'd been destined to marry from the start.

AND as for the ending of this story, it's simple as can be— they *all* lived happily ever after.